"You Make the Angels Cry"

"You Make the Angels Cry"

Story and Pictures by

Denys Cazet

Bradbury Press ★ Scarsdale, New York

Text and illustrations copyright © 1983 by Denys Cazet
Bradbury Press
866 Third Avenue, New York, N.Y. 10022
An affiliate of Macmillan, Inc.
Collier Macmillan Canada, Inc.
Manufactured in the United States of America
2 4 6 8 10 9 7 5 3
The text of this book is set in 16 pt. Century Schoolbook. The illustrations are drawn in ink with watercolor wash, reproduced in full color.
Library of Congress Cataloging in Publication Data
Cazet, Denys.
  "You make the angels cry".
  Summary: When rain begins to fall after his mother scolds him, Albert is convinced that he really made the angels cry.
  [1. Behavior—Fiction] I. Title.
PZ7.C2985Yo   1982   [E]   82-9581
ISBN 0-02-717830-7

For Donna M.

After school one day, Albert waved goodbye to his two best friends and opened the door to his house.

"Hey, Mom!" Albert shouted. "I'm home!"

He reached for the cookie jar but . . .

. . . the wind blew the window open and knocked
the jar over.

The jar bounced off the sink and crashed to the floor.

"Honestly!" said Albert's mother. "Look at this mess!"

"But I didn't . . ."

"No buts about it, Albert," his mother scolded.
"You make the angels cry!"

Albert looked out the window.
It was raining.

He went to his room.

"No buts about it," muttered Albert.
He put on his boots.

He put on his yellow raincoat and his favorite hat
with the red star.

Albert tip-toed down the hall and slipped out the back door.

He crossed the wide, wide meadow . . .

. . . and climbed to the top of the high, high hill.

Albert looked up into the cold sky.
"I'm sorry I made you cry," he shouted, "but the wind did it!"

The sky twitched and the thunder made Albert shake.

Albert waited.
He waited until the sky stopped twitching.
He waited until the thunder rolled away softly.

He waited until it stopped raining.

After the rain stopped, Albert climbed down from
the top of the high, high hill . . .

. . . and crossed the wide, wide meadow to his house.

He opened the back door and walked quietly into the warm kitchen.

"Albert," his mother said, "where have you been?"

"Across the wide, wide meadow to the top of the high, high hill," he said. "I told the angels I was sorry I made them cry but the wind did it!"

Albert's mother put her arms around Albert and
hugged him tightly.
"You make the sun shine." she said.

Albert looked out the window and saw the sun.

"I know," he said.